H.P. LOVECRAFT'S

DAGON

for beginning readers

By R.J. Ivankovic

For John and Helen
and, as always,
Howard and Theodor.

I'm recording these words
under some mental strain.
I've run out of the drug
that was calming my brain.

By the end of tonight
I will surely be dead.

Maybe then I'll escape
all the things in my head.

Though I've tried to forget it,
I want you to know
why I'd leap from this room
to the street down below.

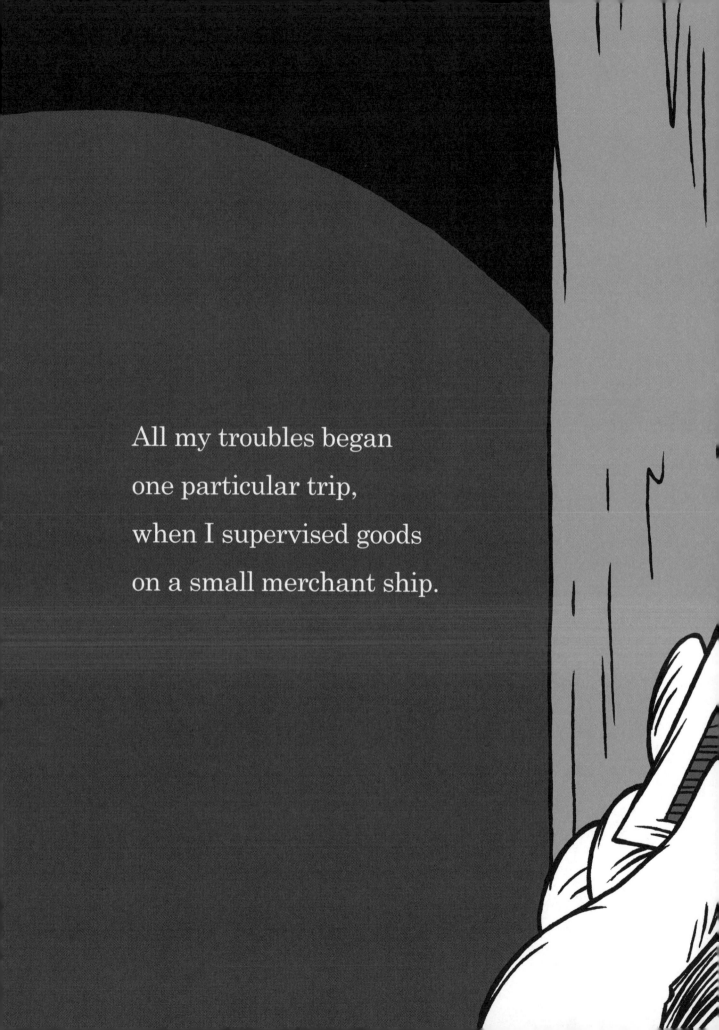

All my troubles began
one particular trip,
when I supervised goods
on a small merchant ship.

As we crossed the Pacific,

unbroken and blue,

we were sailing that ocean

where sailed but a few.

In a stroke of misfortune
we couldn't ignore,
we crossed paths with a ship
from the Kaiser's Great War.

When the sea-raider slowed
and then pulled alongside,
we had no other choice
but to swallow our pride.

We surrendered ourselves
and our ship as a prize.

I began to steal water
and other supplies.

After just a few days,

having kept out of sight,

I escaped in a boat

in the midst of the night.

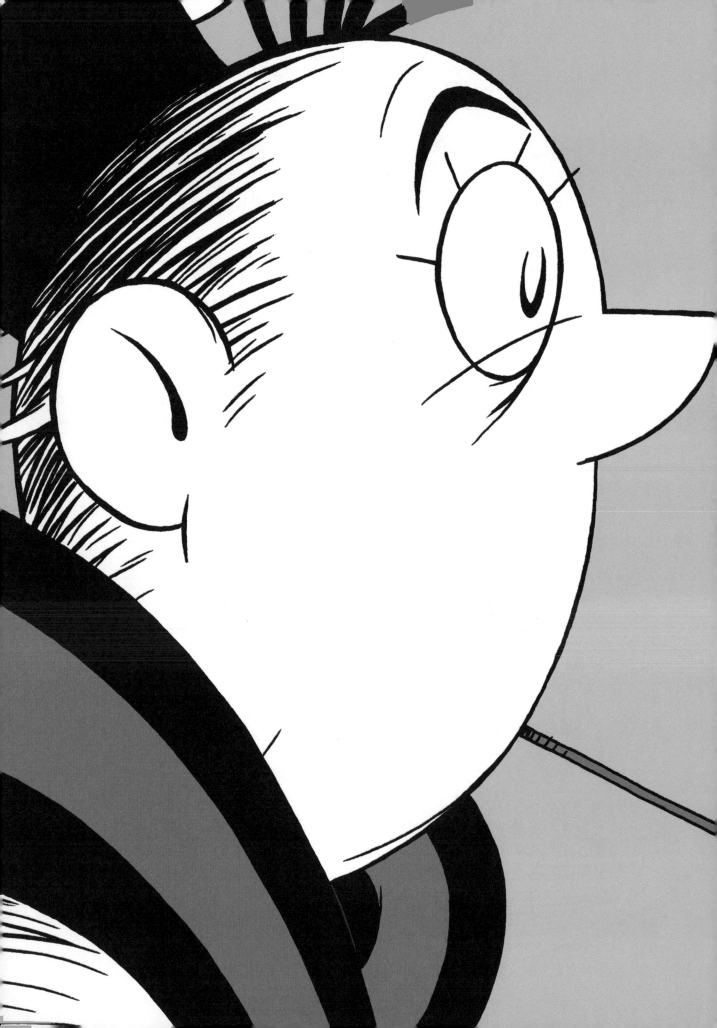

I assumed I would surely
be picked up once more,
or be carried on currents
to some distant shore.

But with no navigator
to show me the way,
the Equator was northward
was all I could say.

After many long days
with no rescue in sight,
I began to lose hope
and had nightmares at night.

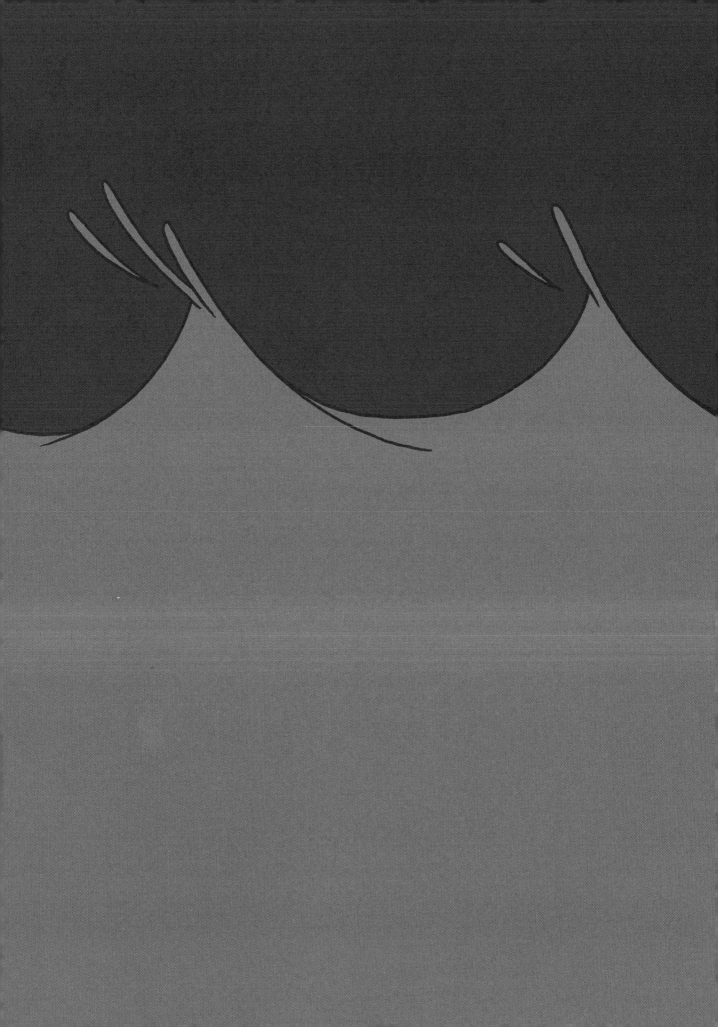

Then one morning I woke
in a scene out of hell.
There were slime and dead fish,
with a sinister smell.

I'm not certain what happened.

It seems so absurd.

I believe a volcanic eruption occurred.

When the hellish black mire
rose up from the deep,
I'd been thrown from the boat
without breaking my sleep.

Having crawled to the boat
like a stranded earthworm,
I sat three days and nights
while the slime was baked firm.

Without sign of the sea

or direction to go,

I felt hopelessly small

in that landscape of woe.

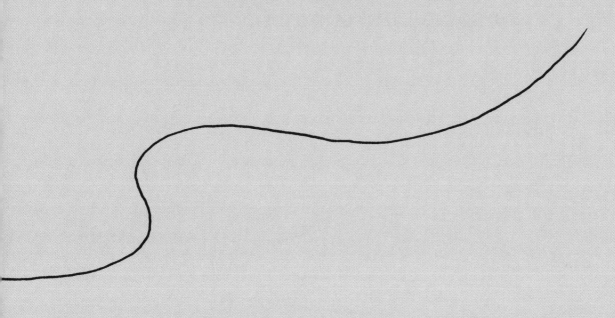

But then off in the distance

I spied a small bump,

that I guessed was a hummock

or some kind of hump.

The monotonous island
showed only that hill.

So I went to explore.

I regret it now, still.

After three days of walking

I paused for a rest,

just before I attempted

my climb to the crest.

Once the chill of the night
had replaced the day's heat,
I discovered a canyon
laid out at my feet.

I climbed into the rift
by the gibbous moonlight,
and I found at the bottom
a breathtaking sight.

In the depths of that canyon
thrown from the sea floor,
there were carvings of things
man has not seen before.

Though the monolith shocked me,

my senses returned,

when the water's dark surface

had rippled and churned.

I was frozen with fear
as the water disgorged
a creature the depths
of the ocean had forged.

When the thing bowed its head
and embraced the cold stone,
all the seeds of the madness
that haunts me were sown.

When it uttered a sound
from the back of its throat,
I succumbed to a panic
and fled to the boat.

Though I tried singing songs
to forget what I'd learned,
I'm not sure I was sane
by the time I'd returned.

I got into the boat
and I lay on the floor.

I heard many strange sounds.

I recall nothing more.

Then the next thing I knew,

I woke up in a bed.

I'd been picked up adrift out at sea,

the nurse said.

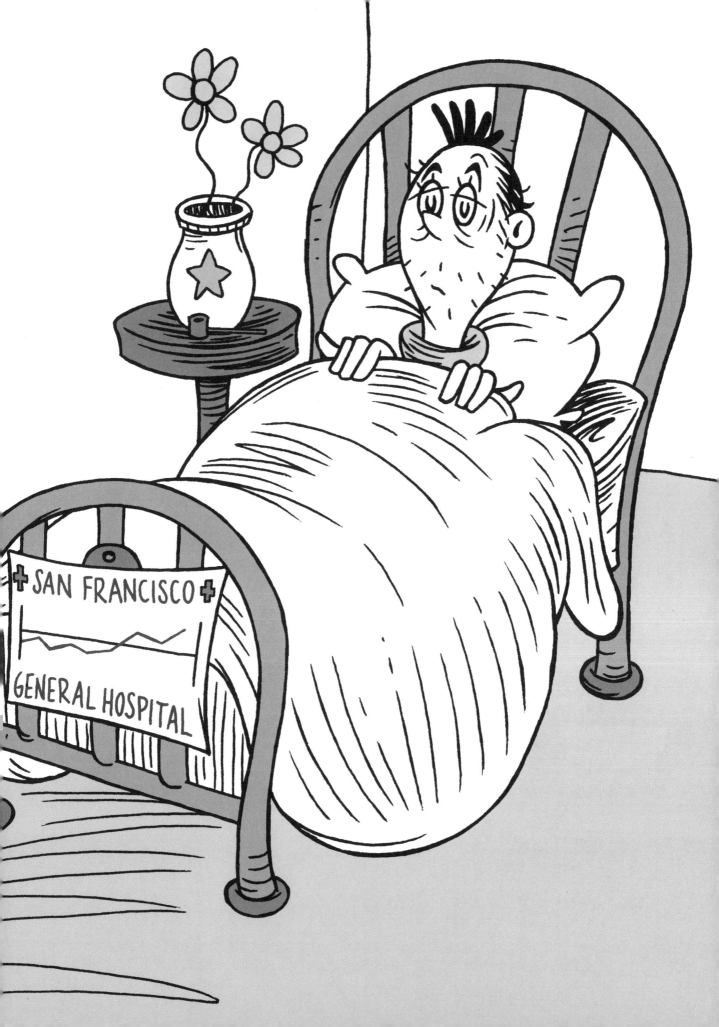

I consulted an expert
to share what I'd seen.

He had no expertise
about where I had been.

So a last word of warning,
for what it is worth:
when the monsters arise
they will conquer the earth.

Now I've run out of time
and can tell you no more,
as the creature's outside
and just thumped on my door!

It has followed me here,
undersea and on land,
in an effort to catch me—

My goodness, *that hand!*

I will not let it find me.

Of that, I've no doubt,

though the window

presents me...

...my only way out.